Arthur the King

Tales of King Arthur

First published in 2006 by
Franklin Watts
338 Euston Road
London
NW1 3BH

Franklin Watts Australia
Hachette Children's Books
Level 17/207 Kent Street
Sydney
NSW 2000

A CIP catalogue record for this book is available
from the British Library.

ISBN (10) 0 7496 6683 8 (hbk)
ISBN (13) 978-0-7496-6683-5 (hbk)
ISBN (10) 0 7496 6695 1 (pbk)
ISBN (13) 978-0-7496-6695-8 (pbk)

Series Editor: Jackie Hamley
Series Advisor: Dr Barrie Wade
Series Designer: Peter Scoulding

Printed in China

Franklin Watts is a division of
Hachette Children's Books.

Arthur
the King

by Karen Wallace and Neil Chapman

W
FRANKLIN WATTS
LONDON•SYDNEY

Arthur was King of Britain, but he still had to fight for his kingdom.

His worst enemy was Lord Pellinor.
"I shall defeat this traitor,"
cried Arthur.

He grabbed a spear and
rode into the forest.

"You are not as strong as
Lord Pellinor," warned Merlin
the magician. "Turn back!"
But Arthur didn't listen.

Arthur charged at Lord Pellinor,
but he broke his own spear.
So he fought with his sword.

Lord Pellinor smashed

Arthur's sword to pieces.

"I will kill you now!" he cried.

Merlin appeared. "If you kill King Arthur, you will destroy Britain," he said.

"King Arthur is a brave knight," said Lord Pellinor. "If he agrees, I will serve him instead."

Arthur was so badly hurt that he heard nothing.

When Arthur woke up, he was safe with Merlin. The magician gave him medicine and healed all his wounds.

"Come with me," said Merlin.
"A king needs a sword." They
rode to the magic land of Avalon.

They stopped at a lake and
stepped into a boat. It floated
into the middle of the water.

Suddenly, the lake turned silver around them. Then an arm appeared with a sword in its hand.

Arthur was amazed.

"Is that for me?" he asked.

"Yes," replied Merlin.

"The sword is called Excalibur."

The boat took them back to their horses. "We will meet Lord Pellinor in the forest," warned Merlin. "Let him pass." "This time I will kill him with Excalibur," cried Arthur.

"No," said Merlin. "He will serve you well and his sons will become your bravest knights.

"Arthur, you must learn how to become a wise king!" Arthur looked longingly at Excalibur and sighed.

"Which do you like better?" asked Merlin. "The sword or this shield?"
"The sword," cried Arthur.

"You are unwise," said Merlin.
"The shield will protect you from
wounds. Carry it always."

At that moment, Lord Pellinor rode past. Merlin wove a spell so he could not see them. Arthur wanted to fight but he stayed where he was.

"Well done," said Merlin. "Remember, things are not always as they appear."

When they arrived at his castle, Arthur showed everyone Excalibur. "You are the bravest knight in the land," cried his knights. "Now, with that sword, you are the most powerful, too!"

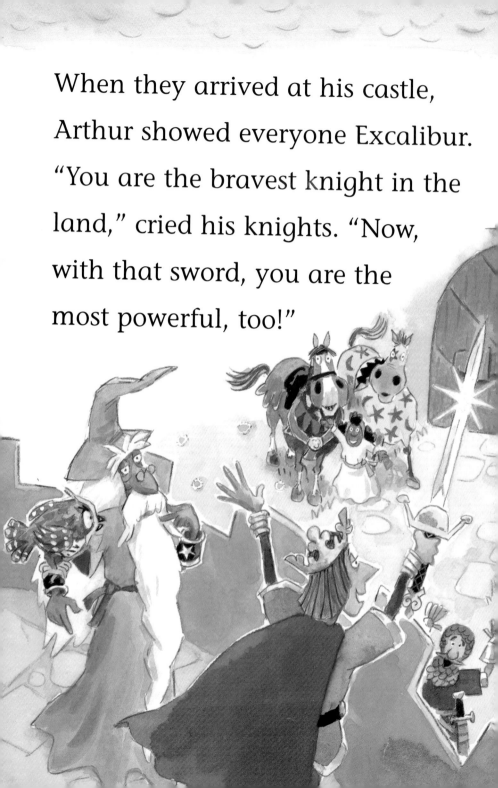

29

With Merlin's help, Arthur grew up to be a wise and powerful king.

And, in time, Lord Pellinor and his sons became some of Arthur's bravest, most loyal knights.

Hopscotch has been specially designed to fit the requirements of the National Literacy Strategy. It offers real books by top authors and illustrators for children developing their reading skills. There are 37 Hopscotch stories to choose from:

Marvin, the Blue Pig
ISBN 0 7496 4619 5

Plip and Plop
ISBN 0 7496 4620 9

The Queen's Dragon
ISBN 0 7496 4618 7

Flora McQuack
ISBN 0 7496 4621 7

Willie the Whale
ISBN 0 7496 4623 3

Naughty Nancy
ISBN 0 7496 4622 5

Run!
ISBN 0 7496 4705 1

The Playground Snake
ISBN 0 7496 4706 X

"Sausages!"
ISBN 0 7496 4707 8

The Truth about Hansel and Gretel
ISBN 0 7496 4708 6

Pippin's Big Jump
ISBN 0 7496 4710 8

Whose Birthday Is It?
ISBN 0 7496 4709 4

The Princess and the Frog
ISBN 0 7496 5129 6

Flynn Flies High
ISBN 0 7496 5130 X

Clever Cat
ISBN 0 7496 5131 8

Moo!
ISBN 0 7496 5332 9

Izzie's Idea
ISBN 0 7496 5334 5

Roly-poly Rice Ball
ISBN 0 7496 5333 7

I Can't Stand It!
ISBN 0 7496 5765 0

Cockerel's Big Egg
ISBN 0 7496 5767 7

How to Teach a Dragon Manners
ISBN 0 7496 5873 8

The Truth about those Billy Goats
ISBN 0 7496 5766 9

Marlowe's Mum and the Tree House
ISBN 0 7496 5874 6

Bear in Town
ISBN 0 7496 5875 4

The Best Den Ever
ISBN 0 7496 5876 2

ADVENTURE STORIES

Aladdin and the Lamp
ISBN 0 7496 6678 1 *
ISBN 0 7496 6692 7

Blackbeard the Pirate
ISBN 0 7496 6676 5 *
ISBN 0 7496 6690 0

George and the Dragon
ISBN 0 7496 6677 3 *
ISBN 0 7496 6691 9

Jack the Giant-Killer
ISBN 0 7496 6680 3 *
ISBN 0 7496 6693 5

TALES OF KING ARTHUR

1. The Sword in the Stone
ISBN 0 7496 6681 1 *
ISBN 0 7496 6694 3

2. Arthur the King
ISBN 0 7496 6683 8 *
ISBN 0 7496 6695 1

3. The Round Table
ISBN 0 7496 6684 6 *
ISBN 0 7496 6697 8

4. Sir Lancelot and the Ice Castle
ISBN 0 7496 6685 4 *
ISBN 0 7496 6698 6

TALES OF ROBIN HOOD

Robin and the Knight
ISBN 0 7496 6686 2 *
ISBN 0 7496 6699 4

Robin and the Monk
ISBN 0 7496 6687 0 *
ISBN 0 7496 6700 1

Robin and the Friar
ISBN 0 7496 6688 9 *
ISBN 0 7496 6702 8

Robin and the Silver Arrow
ISBN 0 7496 6689 7 *
ISBN 0 7496 6703 6

* hardback